Chomps, Flea, and Gray Cat (That's Me!)

Books by Bill Wallace

Red Dog
Trapped in Death Cave

Available from ARCHWAY Paperbacks

Aloha Summer
The Backward Bird Dog
Beauty
The Biggest Klutz in Fifth Grade
Blackwater Swamp
Buffalo Gal
The Christmas Spurs
Danger in Quicksand Swamp
Danger on Panther Peak
    [*Original title:* Shadow on the Snow]
A Dog Called Kitty
Eye of the Great Bear
Ferret in the Bedroom, Lizards in the Fridge
The Final Freedom
Journey into Terror
Never Say Quit
Snot Stew
Totally Disgusting!
True Friends
Upchuck and the Rotten Willy
Upchuck and the Rotten Willy: The Great Escape
Upchuck and the Rotten Willy: Running Wild
Watchdog and the Coyotes

Available from MINSTREL BOOKS

Books by Carol and Bill Wallace

The Flying Flea, Callie, and Me
That Furball Puppy and Me
Chomps, Flea, and Gray Cat (That's Me!)

Available from MINSTREL BOOKS

Books by Nikki Wallace

Stubby and the Puppy Pack

Available from MINSTREL BOOKS

Carol Wallace and Bill Wallace

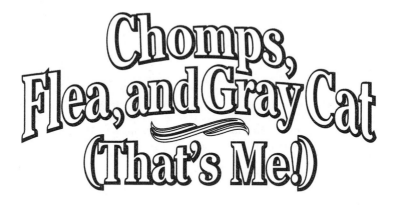

Chomps, Flea, and Gray Cat (That's Me!)

A MINSTREL® HARDCOVER
PUBLISHED BY POCKET BOOKS

New York   London   Toronto   Sydney   Singapore

A MINSTREL HARDCOVER

 A Minstrel Book published by
POCKET BOOKS, a division of Simon & Schuster, Inc.
1230 Avenue of the Americas, New York, NY 10020

ISBN: 0-671-03830-3

First Minstrel Books hardcover printing January 2001

10 9 8 7 6 5 4 3 2 1

A MINSTREL BOOK and colophon are registered trademarks
of Simon & Schuster, Inc.

Printed in the U.S.A.

To
Andrea Paige King and Cassandra Lynn King—
thanks for sharing Rocky with us!!!
And to
Carole Blevins, Cheryl Green, Rhonda Johnston,
Cinde Pearson, Kendra Schenk, Cindy Schmidt,
Cathy Simer and Deloris Smith
for their support and friendship!

CHAPTER 1

I loved sitting in the House Mama's lap!

Trouble was, sometimes we just didn't sit and love. Sometimes—like today—she took the wire brush to me. I guess I needed it. The days were getting longer and warmer. It felt good to get rid of my extra hair. But sometimes the teeth on the brush got stuck.

"Spring must be coming, Gray. The way your winter coat is falling out, warm weather must be right around the corner." Mama yanked a ball of fur from my back. It hurt.

I flinched. My hair's not falling out, I thought. You're pulling it out! Twisting my body, I tried to get away from her.

"Sorry, Gray. But if we don't get these knots out, your fur will mat up. I'm trying to be careful!"

Each time Mama stroked me with the brush, she ran her hand along my soft fur to help take the sting out. I struggled to get away, but she kept a firm hold on me.

Chomps bounded in and put his front paws on the couch while Mama finished my grooming. His ears stood straight up. He tilted his head to one side.

"You look funny, Gray." Chomps turned his head the other direction to get a closer look at what Mama was doing.

I stuck my nose in the air and flipped my tail. "You don't look so good yourself, Chomps."

He just smiled at me and started to bark. "Let's play!" The pile of white fur bounced around the couch.

Mama started brushing again. She held me firmly with one hand while she ran the brush from my neck to the very tip of me.

"Ah, come on, Gray. I want to play really bad!"

"Can't you see what's happening here? Or do you have too much white fluff covering your eyes to tell that I can't get away?"

The pup bounced even more as Mama finished brushing me.

"Get back, Chomps! I'm almost done. Then you can both go outside." Mama lifted me in the air with both hands and looked me over. She gave me a hug and headed for the door.

"Come on, pup, you can go out now. I have to run

to the store, and you guys can get a little sunshine."

Mama scooted Chomps out the door with her foot. She set me down on the porch swing. I ruffled and jerked my fur a few times to get rid of the sting from the brushing. Mama jingled her keys as she walked to the driveway.

"Be good animals. I'll be right back."

The sound of the car's motor roared, coughed, then sputtered as Mama drove away.

Chomps walked to the end of the porch and sat down with his nose to the wind. The strong breeze shook his shaggy fur.

Chomps was very new to the place. He had arrived at Christmas. Mama called him a Scottish terrier. She said that he was wheaton color. That meant he was sort of white, not black like most Scotties are supposed to be. I guess that Chomps was okay. We had become pretty good friends.

I smiled while I watched the little puppy snap at flies that buzzed around. Fact is, that's how he had gotten his name. When the Daddy would scuffle and play with him, Chomps would pretend to bite. When his teeth popped together, they made a loud, funny, chomping sound. Mama and Daddy thought it was pretty neat to have a little bitty fluff ball make such a big noise.

When he first came to live with us, I didn't like him very much. He was wild, he had no manners, and he smelled like a puppy. I tried to get rid of the little furball by helping him mess up the kitchen one night. It worked. But instead of just putting the puppy outside for a bit, the Mama and Daddy made a bed in the barn for Chomps.

There were rats in the barn.

They were big, hairy, and they had really sharp teeth. I felt so bad about what I had done, I had to go rescue him. There were too many rats. Callie, the old cat who lives with us, brought the People to our rescue—just in the nick of time. Thinking about those horrible rats sent a chill up my back.

"Let's play." Chomps barked. When he did, I jumped. He looked up at me. I swished my tail in front of his furry face.

"Okay, I want to play chase. I'll be it first!" I said.

The short puppy legs churned as he tried to run from me. He only made it to the end of the porch when I swatted him on the head. "You're it!"

I fluffed my fur and ran to the base of the tree. I looked back. The pup was still standing where I had left him. He was trying to get his stubby legs moving, but all they did was spin on the concrete.

I scooted up the tree to the bottom branch. I sharpened my claws while I waited for Chomps to catch up with me.

As soon as he got to the tree, I jumped over him, landed on the ground, and ran to the lilac bushes. Chomps spun around and chased after me. When he got near, I did a back flip, landed on top of him, and rolled him into a ball. Then I took off. The dog gave a little shake and came after me. Sliding to a stop, I turned on him and flattened my chest to the ground. With my rear in the air, I swished my tail and growled deep in my throat.

Chomps just wagged his tail. "I'm not afraid of you, Gray."

The little pup swatted me on the head. "You're it again!"

I pounced and flipped him a second time. Chomps shook his little body and tried to clear his head before he ran straight for me.

Just as he closed in, I dodged to the side. The dog tried to turn. He was still young and clumsy, so he slipped. He rolled over about three times. I swished my tail and strutted up to him. "Get up, Chomps. You're it!"

The silly dog kept chasing me and knocking himself to the ground. He was back up each time with more energy. Chomps was always ready to play chase. When I finally had enough, I jumped to the porch swing. The pup stood below me and looked up with his shaggy, hairy face.

"Let's play some more."

I curled up in the corner of the swing. "Later, pup. You've worn me out."

Chomps put his front paws on the swing. "Tell me about the bird again. I can't believe that you have a bird for a friend." The dog stared at me.

"Okay, but then I need to get in a catnap."

I told him about the Mockingbird Mother who lived in the apple tree. She was a good mother, but one of her babies was slow to leave the nest. When it came time for all the mockingbirds to go south for the winter, one little bird stayed behind. She almost starved to death before she jumped from the tree and landed on my back. I named her Flea because she was so hard to get rid of. It was lots of fun helping her catch grasshoppers and learn how to fly. The trouble was, she was afraid of high places. Callie came up with an idea. With a little help from Bullsnake, the snake who lived in the woodpile, we finally convinced the bird that she could fly. I still miss her. I wish spring would hurry so my friend would come back.

I had told Chomps the story of Flea lots of times. He didn't seem to understand that a cat and a bird could be friends.

Warm moist breezes made me sleepy. Chomps finally curled up to take a nap, too. Suddenly his ears shot up. They were so long and pointed. They reminded me of a jackrabbit's.

"Hey, Gray. Here comes Mama!"

I perked my ears trying to figure out what Chomps heard. "How do you know? I don't hear anything."

"I recognize the noise from the car," he said. "It is

struggling to get up the hill. Mama is almost on the dirt road near the creek."

I strained my ears and leaned toward the direction that Chomps was looking. I still couldn't hear anything except the wind.

I finally heard the sputtering sounds as the car chugged up the road that led to the house.

When Mama parked in the driveway, she got out and began talking to the old car. She yelled at it, like she did when Chomps missed the newspapers on the kitchen floor. He did that a lot when he was little. When Chomps heard the tone of her voice, his ears flattened and his tail tucked under his tummy.

Another sound came to my ears. The noisy tractor was coming up the driveway. Mama stood at the back of the car. Fists on her hips, she watched Daddy get closer to the house.

Chomps perked his ears up again. His fluffy tail wagged, but he didn't move from the end of the porch.

"I'm so sick of this rattletrap. It wouldn't start when I tried to leave the grocery store. I had to call Jim at the car dealership. He drove all the way across town to start the old thing for me. Jim says it's about on its last legs." Mama sighed and shook her head. "We also need to talk to the county commissioner about this road. We haven't even had a good rain yet, and it's almost impossible to get through the low-water crossing at the creek."

"Here, Kay, let me help you get this stuff in. I think you need to sit awhile. It sounds like you had a pretty bad day, and you only went to the grocery store."

Daddy helped Mama get the bags out of the car, but he had to slam the back door to get it to stay shut.

As they came closer to the front door, Chomps wagged his tail so fast that his whole body shook. Mama picked him up.

"You guys make me happy." Mama smiled down at me. "What are you going to do, Gray? Want to come in?"

I rubbed against Mama's leg to let her know I was happy to see her, but I walked to the end of the sidewalk.

"Okay, just asking." Mama carried Chomps into the house. "I'll let Callie come out with you for a while."

I was still tired from the puppy romp. Callie would take a nice quiet nap with me. I would go on a trophy hunt later.

CHAPTER 2

When Mama finally brought Callie out, the old cat went straight to the rocking chair and hopped up. She sat for a long time sniffing the smells of early spring. She washed her paws and face before finally curling her tail around her body and going to sleep. I jumped up on the swing. Taking long strokes with my tongue, I tried to wash the fur on my chest. Chunks of winter hair came out. Rubbing my tongue against the roof of my mouth, I tried to get rid of the fuzzy stuff. Then I shook my head trying to get the furball out of my mouth.

I finally gave up and flopped down on the towel Mama had placed on the swing. My whiskers twitched as I watched the birds taking turns at the feeder filled with sunflower seeds. I closed my eyes and dreamed of warm summer days.

The squeak of the front door startled me as Mama put Chomps down on the concrete near the swing. She patted him on the head, then closed the door behind her.

The pup looked up at me with his little shiny eyes. "Let's play!" He started bouncing around below me.

I tucked my front legs tighter to my body. He made little yipping sounds that made me blink.

"Not now, pup. Cats need lots of sleep." I closed my eyes, but the puppy sounds continued.

"Dogs need exercise! Let's play!"

"Later, pup." I hoped that he would get the hint. "Why didn't Mama exercise you?"

"I tried to get her to play, but she just wanted me to sit still under her feet. She was in the office working. She said you'd play with me."

"Later, pup."

I tried to catch a few minutes of sleep, but Chomps just kept on and on. I finally stretched my legs out and washed my paws. Another hairball stuck in my mouth.

I stood up, then jumped down to the concrete. Callie was still asleep in the chair. The pup probably did need some exercise, and I could do a little trophy hunting.

I motioned him with a jerk of my head.

"Okay, pup, but you're going to have to follow some rules. We're going to go down to the hayfield.

We'll play, but you have to do some watching first."

Chomps's ears stood straight up as he listened to me. "I'll watch."

"I'm serious, Chomps. I'm going to teach you how to hunt. You have to promise to be very quiet and stay back until I have a trophy for the Mama."

The pup's ears stayed straight up, but his tail began to wag even harder. "I'll be good, Gray. I promise."

We walked through the yard and down the dirt road. The pasture in front of the house was damp from the morning dew. We crossed the road, then crawled under the fence. Chomps bounced and hopped over big clumps of grass.

I looked back at the pup. "Be quiet, Chomps. I have to listen for mice."

He sat very still as I flattened my body to the ground. I kept my ears perked, listening for the mice scurrying under the dead grass. Suddenly I popped up and came down on my first catch. I brought my prize back and laid it in front of the pup.

"See how easy that was, Chomps."

He frowned at the mouse. His long ears wobbled back and forth. Finally he looked up and gave me a goofy smile.

"Can you show me that again?" he asked.

Crouching down, I perked my ears, listening. I pounced at the sound that I heard in the grass. I missed. My tail flipped one way and then the other.

A sound came from my left side this time. I crouched and held my breath. I missed again.

I turned around and glared at Chomps. "Would you be quiet?" I hissed.

His eyes popped wide and his little mouth fell open. "I didn't do anything," he whimpered. "I didn't bark. I didn't move. I didn't even breathe deep."

My tail gave another jerk. This time it went straight up. "Uh . . . well . . ." I stammered. "Just keep it that way."

This mouse was way too lucky. I strolled farther out into the field. . . .

Chomps's tail wagged all over the place when I sat my trophy down in front of him. He looked at it. He sniffed it. He even clunked it with his paw.

"Think you're ready to try it now?" I asked.

He nodded his head so hard his ears flopped. "Sure! That looks easy. I bet I can do that."

Head high on one end and tail high on the other, Chomps strutted out into the field. His ears twitched and wiggled. All at once he stopped. He crouched low, then he leaped in the air. He landed about a foot from the mouse.

"Slow down, pup. You have to listen, then think about where it's going to go next. Don't pounce until you know for sure which way the mouse is headed."

Chomps pawed the dirt in front of him and bounced backward as he barked at the spot where he thought the mouse was. I felt my eyes roll.

Suddenly he jumped again. This time he went straight up. Trouble was, his front feet jumped harder than his back feet. Somehow while he was in midair, he got off balance. When he came down, his back end was way ahead of his front end. His hind paws touched the ground, then his tail hit, then he flopped—flat on his back.

I guess there was a low spot where he landed. He tried to roll one way, but he couldn't, so he tried to roll the other. The little puppy looked totally silly, squirming on his back with his little stubby legs churning in the air.

Still upside down, he scrunched his head back so that he could look at me. "I thought I had it."

My eyes rolled again, but I blinked and caught myself before Chomps saw me. I sighed, then took a deep breath.

"It's okay. I didn't catch the first mouse I chased. It just takes patience and practice. Now get up and try it again."

"I can't. I'm stuck!" He flopped back and forth a few times until he finally got to his feet.

His ears perked up as he put his nose to the ground and moved slowly toward the smells in the hay. He pounced again. This time he slid and bumped his chin on the ground. Dried grass and hay stuck to his fluffy hair as he tried to shake himself clean.

Chomps worked for a long time practicing his

hunting skills. He learned to keep his nose close to the ground and his eyes stayed locked on one spot until he was ready to spring. But his pouncing still wasn't very good. He would fall on his nose, trip himself and do a somersault, or spin around until he got dizzy. At least he didn't get stuck on his back again.

I guess for a dog—I mean a puppy—it wasn't all that bad. At least he tried hard.

I finally decided it was time to head back to the house. The little dog was tired and his fur was full of dirt, grass, and stickers.

"Shake yourself, Chomps. You need to get that stuff out of your hair or Mama will know that we have been away from the yard."

The pup tried to get the mess off. Each shake seemed to make his curly fur even tighter. The clay dirt made red spots.

As we headed back to the house, the pup would stop and try to pull stickers and twigs out with his teeth. He stopped, sat down, and reached around to tug at something. Only when he stood up, more junk was stuck to the side he had been sitting on. It took forever to get back to the yard.

As we neared the front door, we both knew that we were in trouble. Mama was standing on the porch. With her hands on her hips, she scowled at us. When Chomps saw her, his tail drooped. His ears flattened against his head. Mama walked over to him and picked him up. They disappeared into the house.

Callie's whiskers twitched as she stretched her front legs. "Boy, you've done it now! Mama is really mad at Chomps. She's been looking for him for an hour. Where did you take him? To the creek?"

"We were just hunting in the field. He's going to be a good hunter with a little more practice. Well, maybe lots more practice."

"He won't get *any* more practice. Mama will probably only let him out in the backyard from now on. She was worried about him. He's too little to be very far from the house by himself."

"He wasn't by himself. *I* was with him."

Callie flipped her tail. "I don't think that Mama counts you."

I frowned at her. "But I took good care of him. I brought him home, didn't I?"

Callie didn't answer. She walked to the door and lay down on the mat.

Just then I realized that I had forgotten to bring a trophy home for Mama!

CHAPTER 3

It was evening before I saw Chomps again. When Daddy came home, and opened the door, I slipped inside between his feet. He never even noticed me. I searched the house looking for that dog. Mama had him in the bathroom. I could hear the roar of the hairdryer. The door was open just a bit. I pushed my cheek against it until it opened wide enough for me to slip in. Mama sat on the floor. Chomps shivered on a towel in front of her. His wet fur lay flat against his body. Mama tried to hold him with her elbows as she used the brush and the hairdryer to clean up the messy dog.

"What are you doing, Gray? Do you want some of this?" She turned the air toward me.

I jumped back and darted out the door.

I had met the hairdryer before.

I slid under the bed and started cleaning my fur. I already had most of the junk out, but I could still find little chunks of knotted hair around stickers.

I perked up my ears when Mama took Chomps out of the bathroom. They headed for the front part of the house. Mama had put cardboard boxes between the kitchen and the dining room. The People could step over them, but Chomps wasn't able to escape. I jumped over the boxes with one hop. The poor pup was sitting in the middle of a pile of dry towels.

"Hey, pup. Sorry about the bath. I thought that we would get back without getting caught."

"She yanked most of my hair out! Am I bald?" The pup looked down at his fluffy fur. "She said I had a sack of trash connected to me. She said my curly hair grabbed every sticker in the field. What wouldn't come out, Mama pulled out!"

"You look fine. I don't see any skin showing at all. We'll have to be more careful the next time we go out." I backed away from the pup when Mama stepped toward the sink.

"Gray, what kind of mischief are you up to? Scat, I'm not very happy with you right now." Mama shoved me toward the cardboard with her foot.

I flipped my tail as I jumped over the boxes and strolled into the living room to take my bath on the couch.

Mama stepped over the boxes and sat down at the

table with Daddy. "Owen, what are we going to do about that car? Every time I think it can't get any worse, something else happens to it!"

"Maybe it just needs some new spark plugs."

"I don't think that spark plugs are the answer this time!" Mama threw a towel at Daddy. "Didn't Jim put new spark plugs in last month?"

Daddy shrugged and nodded his head. "Yeah, I think he did."

Daddy sat there for a moment. Finally he smiled and reached out to hold Mama's hand. "I guess that we do need to think about a new car. The old one has been pretty good, but it's on its last legs. It costs as much to keep it running as new car payments would. We've had two good years with the wheat."

He stopped and scratched his chin. Then he looked at Mama. His smile got even bigger. "Do you want to go car shopping tomorrow?"

Mama let out a little squeal. It made my ears perk straight up. I looked around. Mama grabbed Daddy and kissed him on the head. "Do I? I can't wait!"

"I think I can spare a little time tomorrow. Maybe all day. We need to get a better car for that road. There's no guarantee they'll get the work done soon."

All day? I got up from the couch and hopped over the cardboard to get to Chomps. The little dog was crouched in the pile of towels. I could barely see his black eyes under the mop of fur. "Hey, pup. Why are you being so still?"

"I'm afraid that Mama will hunt for new burrs and stickers in my fur."

I tried to look him over. I didn't see anything that Mama would want to mess with. "I think you're safe for a while. We are going out again tomorrow when Mama and Daddy go to town. They said that they would be gone *all day*. We can hunt some more. I think you are going to be pretty good with practice."

"I don't know. Mama wasn't very happy when we got home today. She stuck me in a box until she gave me that bath. I'm afraid to move. I'm afraid she'll get me again." Chomps was still shaking.

"Just be good for the rest of the day, and I think Mama will forget about what happened. You had fun today didn't you?"

Chomps peeked up at me. "I don't know if it was *that* fun or not!"

Mama scooped me up about that time. "Gray, you need some more outside time. Look at the furballs you left on the couch. I don't have time to brush you right now."

All at once I was on the front porch. My whiskers blew back against my face as Mama shut the door behind me. I had time to get a trophy before dark. My tail in the air, I walked down the sidewalk toward the apple tree.

I looked up at the place where the nest had been last year. Still no sign of Mama Mockingbird or Flea. I sharpened my claws on the trunk.

The door to the barn was open just enough for me to get inside. I really wanted to see what was there, but something told me to stay away. I stepped carefully to the doorway and poked my head through the opening. My ears were up as I looked about. Shadows filled the spaces around the hay bales inside the barn. I crouched low as I listened for the sounds of mice and rats. Beady eyes blinked back at me. Then I saw the familiar shape of a big rat. Nora was eating grain in the corner. An evil glint of light came from her eye. She didn't stop eating, but her yellow teeth glistened as she turned toward me. I remembered the time that the rats almost got Chomps and me.

My legs suddenly felt wobbly as I tried to back out of the barn. I would return some other time. I looked back and the big rat gave me a sneaky grin. I shuddered as I hurried from the barn.

I raced to the front door of the house.

"MEOW! Let me in!" The air was getting warm, but I still felt a chill from being in the barn. I scratched at the screen door.

"Gray! What's going on, cat?"

As soon as the door opened, I darted in and scampered to the safe place under the bed. I could hear Callie's gentle breathing above me. I finally crawled

out and looked up. I could see the tips of her ears. The old cat was asleep on a pillow. I leaped to the bed beside her.

"Hey, Callie, are you awake?" I purred. "Callie?"

"I wasn't asleep. I was only catnapping. What's the matter with you?" The old cat stretched out her front paws and began washing her face. I felt my fur ripple.

"I've been out in the barn, and those creepy rats are still there. Don't they go some place in the spring?"

Without stopping her bath, Callie looked toward the door. "What rats?"

"Those barn rats. The ones that nearly got Chomps and me when it was so cold. Remember, you brought the House People to get the puppy out of trouble."

Pulling her paws in under her chest, Callie shook her head. "Those rats. Yes, when the weather gets warmer, they begin to move around outside more. If they have a free meal, though, they'll stay until they've cleaned the barn out."

I felt my heart drop. "Callie. I'm afraid of those rats, especially that big one called Nora. When she looks at me, all I can see are those big yellow teeth inside that sneaky grin. It makes me feel all jittery. I just want to run and hide."

"Where are you going to hide? Under the bed? You'll get tired of being down there with all those

she clipped. "What a lovable little puppy you are, Chompies. You're such a nice little fellow. You can come in any time. What a sweetheart." His tail wagged so hard it shook him clear up to his pointy ears.

I couldn't take any more. I curled up in a ball and tried to catch a quick catnap before I got sick. The sounds of barking dogs, clippers, and hairdryers were soon gone from my head as I dreamed of mice racing away from me.

"We have Chompers and Gray ready." Amy stood near the front of the shop talking to herself. She held a white thing against the side of her head. I had seen Mama do the same thing, but for the life of me I couldn't figure out why she had so much fun talking to herself. "Yes, you can pick them up any time."

Chomps was in the cage next to me, but I couldn't see anything but some white fur.

It wasn't long before Mama came in to get us. Jeff carried Chomps's cage to the car and Mama carried mine. Before she closed the back door, she stopped and looked at us.

"Chomps, you look so grown-up. What a big dog you are." I could hear his tail hitting the side of the cage.

"Aren't you cute, Gray? Did you enjoy your beauty shop visit? You look so pretty." I rubbed my the desk. Papers scattered. My feet slipped, but I managed to catch myself. Some of the papers fluttered as they fell to the carpet.

"Gray! For goodness' sakes, can't I have just a few more minutes?" Mama picked me up and set me back on the floor.

I rubbed my cheek against her leg. I really loved Mama and wanted her to know it. I guess I rubbed a little too hard because one of my teeth scraped across her ankle.

"Ouch! Come on, Gray, give me a break. I'm almost done."

"Be patient, Gray. She won't forget us now," Callie purred.

The sounds of Daddy's tractor got Chomps excited. He jumped up from his place on Mama's feet and scampered to the back door. Mama followed him.

"Chomps, do you need out?" she called. We chased after Mama and Chomps. He bounced against the door, and she opened the screen for him. Chomps shot out as Daddy was coming in. He almost tripped over the little furball. Before Chomps could get turned around and charge back inside the house, Daddy closed the door.

"Are you almost ready?" he asked.

"As soon as I feed these animals, I will be. I have found the answer to our car problems." Mama pushed the lever on the can opener.

"Meow!"

Callie and I got separate bowls of food. Yum!

Mama fixed Chomps a little bowl of dry food and took it out to the yard. "Chomps will have to stay in the pen to keep him from running off like he did yesterday."

By the time Mama was ready to leave, I had already taken a quick catnap.

"Let's go, Gray. You and Callie can get some sunshine while we are gone." She scooped me up and set me outside. Callie was already on the porch swing. I crawled under it to roll in the concrete dust.

Mama and Daddy closed the door and walked toward the driveway.

The old car roared, sputtered, and chugged away.

As soon as I couldn't hear it anymore, I strolled to the end of the driveway. The car was nowhere in sight. I walked back toward Callie.

I put my paws on the swing. "Hey, Callie. How long does it take to hunt a car? Do you have to be quiet like when you hunt mice? Do you have to sneak up and pounce?"

Callie opened one eye. "No. It's a different kind of hunting."

I frowned and tilted my head to the side.

Callie opened the other eye, then blinked. "Okay, Gray. Remember back at Christmastime, before all the people came. Mama went hunting for things at the store. She calls it shopping. When she finds things, it makes her just as proud and happy as we feel when we catch a mouse."

"Does it make Daddy happy, too?"

"No, it just makes him grumpy."

"So? Will they be back really quick?"

Callie shook her head, then closed her eyes once more. "No, shopping for a car is like big-time hunting. They'll probably be gone all day."

My whiskers sprang up on both sides of my face. "Oh, boy!"

Callie peeked down at me. "What are you up to Gray?"

"Just going on an adventure," I purred.

"You better not take that dog with you. You were lucky that Mama and Daddy didn't lock *you* in the cat carrier. They were very upset when they couldn't find Chomps yesterday."

"Relax, Callie. That little fuzzball needs a few hunting lessons. He's doing great—for a dog. We're just going for a little practice." I hopped up on the swing.

"Go ahead. But remember, I warned you!"

"Okay, but I need a little help." I curled up near the old cat.

"Forget it, Gray. I'm too old to teach a *dog* how to hunt." Callie blinked sleepily.

"That's not it. I need help getting him out of that pen in the backyard."

Callie's eyes opened wide. "Forget it, Cat! I'm not going to have anything to do with this."

"I just need a little help. He can squeeze through the yard gate if I can get him out of the little pen."

"Sorry, Gray, you're on your own." Callie flipped over and curled up the other way.

I hopped off the swing and headed for the backyard. I'd figure out something on my own.

I looked at the little pen the dog was trapped in. The sides were held up with metal posts. The doghouse was the only back that it had. If we could just squeeze that little pup through the tiny space between the wire side and the doghouse, we were ready to go.

"I'm trapped," Chomps moaned.

"Don't worry, you can get out of there." I tried to encourage the little dog. "All you have to do is shove against this side. You can push this nail loose pretty easy. I don't think that Daddy did a very good job on the pen. He must have been in a hurry."

The little dog tried to shove his way out. He bounced against the side, but nothing happened. He yapped at it but it still wouldn't work. Finally I decided that we would have to dig him out. I started on the outside, while he dug from the inside. At first, he wasn't a very good digger, but he was having so much fun that the hole got bigger and deeper anyway. It wasn't long until his dirty little nose pushed up to meet the hole that I had made on the outside.

As soon as he squeezed his body out, we headed for the gate opening. The place where the gates swung together was easy to push through. We ran for the field. Chomps bounced and hopped around as we trotted past the apple tree. I made him stop while I climbed up to see if I could spot any sign of my bird friends.

I scampered down, clunked the mutt on the head with my paw, then shot up the trunk of the tree once more. Crawling to the end of the first limb, I looked at Chomps.

"You can't get me!" I flattened my ears as I teased the pup.

"Quit playing, Gray. I want to go hunt." Chomps barked at me.

I climbed down the tree and headed for the hay-field. Chomps ran and yipped behind me. The early morning sun seemed to move between the fluffy white clouds in the east.

"Remember, Chomps, you have to follow some rules. You have to be quiet and let me hunt first. You watch, then you will have your chance."

CHAPTER 5

We walked across the pasture, heading for the hay-field. Chomps raced around and jumped as we got close to the road.

"Stop, Chomps! You have to be careful when you go across. Not many cars go by here, but when they do, they usually are going too fast to stop for animals."

Chomps paused and looked back at me. He waited at the edge of the road until I could catch up. I showed the little dog how to look carefully in both directions. I made him hold his breath and listen.

"If you don't see anything and if you don't hear anything, then it's okay to go."

His ears flopped when he nodded his head.

The hunt began about the same as before. Chomps jumped and scampered after sounds that he *thought* he heard in the stiff grass. I watched him. It was easier to let him get some of the energy out of his system before we started any serious hunting.

I finally decided that maybe we should just explore the hill. The mice were doing a good job of hiding anyway.

Chomps ran ahead of me. Suddenly he stopped, spun around, and raced back as quickly as his stubby little legs would carry him. I couldn't believe how fast he was coming at me. My whiskers twitched when I saw how big his eyes were.

"Gray! Hurry!" he yapped.

"What?"

"It's huge!" he said, his eyes growing even bigger. "Makes the ones in the barn look like babies, and he's scared of me. He's running away."

"What?" I repeated. I realized that Chomps was coming so fast that he wouldn't be able to stop. I scrunched down close to the ground, closed my eyes, and braced myself.

Sure enough, the pup slammed into me, fell over, and tumbled about three times. When he scrambled to his feet, he didn't even slow down long enough to shake the grass from his fur. He just charged. This time he jumped over me instead of falling.

"Come on, Gray! It will take both of us to carry him to the mat."

"Chomps, what in the world are you talking about?"

"The trophy!" He didn't even take the time to

glance over his shoulder at me. "It's the biggest trophy ever! Mama won't believe it. She will be so proud of us. It's the most humongous rat I've ever seen in my whole life."

I guess—to a puppy—the animal looked like a big rat. It was sort of gray and it had a long ratty tail. I clamped my lips shut to keep from laughing as Chomps barked and barked at it.

The opossum stood its ground and hissed. Chomps hopped and leaped around yipping until I thought he would knock himself over. I felt my eyes roll. The creature suddenly took off toward the creek. Chomps made small jumps at the opossum's heels as they ran. At the stream the animal stopped, bared his teeth, and hissed again. Chomps's eyes flashed and he stumbled over himself when he ran backward.

"Let's go, Chomps. You don't want him. He isn't going to hurt anything." I flipped my tail and moved toward the meadow.

"But he's a giant trophy! He's a rat and . . ."

"He's not a rat. He's an opossum."

"A what?"

"Never mind. He's not a rat. Just come on."

Chomps started toward me, still keeping an eye on the opossum. Suddenly the animal darted toward the water. Chomps charged him again, growling and making that chomping sound with his jaws. The opossum fell over in a heap.

Chomps's ears shot straight up. His head tilted to one side. Cautiously he leaned toward the animal and nudged him with his nose. He jumped back. When the opossum didn't move, Chomps shoved him again.

Chomps looked back at me. "Is he dead? I didn't do anything!"

"Don't worry. He's okay. Opossums play dead so that their enemies will leave them alone. As soon as we get away and he knows that he is safe, he will sneak off and forget all about us."

Chomps nudged the thing one more time before he followed me toward the hill.

Just as we settled into a nice pace, Chomps suddenly sniffed the air and took off running toward the creek. I perked my ears and tried to sniff the breeze to see what he was so interested in. I froze in fear as I suddenly realized what the little dog had found this time.

Chomps's short stubby legs raced at full speed toward the striped kitty. My whole body tensed. "Chomps! No! It's a skunk! If he sprays you, it will take two weeks for the smell to go away and . . ."

The dumb mutt slid to a stop. He sneezed a couple of times, then spun and raced back to me. We were just lucky he smelled the varmint before it sprayed him.

"Man, that guy *stinks!*" He sneezed again.

"No kidding." I nodded. "See how he's got his tail up? If he sprayed you, *you'd* stink."

"It looked like a black-and-white kitty cat. You and Callie are fun to play with, and I just wanted to have a little chase game."

"We're exploring today, dog. If you want a chase game with a cat, we can go back to the house and play in the yard."

The little dog's ears flattened against his head. "I'd rather explore. I'll try to be careful."

I swished my tail and we headed for the creek.

There was only a trickle of water in the stream. I jumped over. Chomps managed to get one paw muddy when he sloshed through the water. I had to wait for him while he washed his paw. That dumb pup was always washing his feet. When he was done, he raced ahead of me. We hadn't gone very far from the water when he stopped and began barking and bouncing again.

"What now, dog?" My tail flipped so hard, I had to move my hind legs to keep it from knocking me off balance. We would never make it to the rock hill at this rate.

"I saw that rock move! It's got legs!" Chomps barked at the rock again.

"Chomps! It's only a turtle."

"It looks like a rock, but *I* saw it move! If it moved, it will play with me." The mutt just hopped and yipped.

I walked around to the other side. "Look! Here is its head. He has it tucked under his shell. If he decided to come out and get hold of your nose, you wouldn't think it was playing. Come on." The dog circled the turtle a few more times before he finally followed me.

The raindrop hit right between my ears. It was so big and fell so hard that it made my head bob. Blinking, I looked up at the sky. The huge gray clouds swept in from the west. They were dark and scary looking.

Cats are always alert and aware of our surroundings. We are good about keeping an eye on what's going on around us. Nothing ever sneaks up on us cats. Trouble was, I had been so busy watching the crazy pup that I hadn't even seen it coming. Now the storm was right on top of us.

Another drop landed in front of me. It splashed water and dust up onto my whiskers. A huge one hit Chomps, right at the base of his tail. We'd never make it back home before the storm hit. It was too close. With a jerk of my tail, I motioned Chomps to follow. We scampered for the rock overhang.

The storm broke limbs and shook tender leaf buds to the ground. Water ran from the hill toward the creek in small rivers. The rain fell so hard and fast that the rock overhang where we huddled was almost like hiding behind a waterfall. There was lightning and thunder and rain that seemed to last forever. When it all finally rumbled away beyond the far hills, we decided that it was safe to leave our shelter.

The fresh smell of rain filled the air as we walked toward the creek. The sound of running water came to my ears. The creek was no longer a trickle. Water and mud churned and tumbled as it rushed to fill the bed from bank to bank.

"Listen, dog," I said, looking over my shoulder. "You have to do exactly what I say and step exactly where I step. The creek is full. It's muddy and yucky. It's dangerous, too. You have to mind me and listen to everything I say or we could be in trouble. "Okay?"

"Okay." His tail wagged.

"Promise?"

"Promise."

Callie saw us coming from the front porch. She stood up when I got close and swished her tail. "What's wrong with you, Gray?"

"Nothing!" I hissed. "What makes you think something's wrong?"

Callie tilted her head to one side and shrugged her ears. "Oh, no reason. You're just all fuzzed up and your face looks like you've been chewing on a rotten mouse or something. That's all."

I felt my eyes narrow when I saw Chomps appear at the edge of the pine trees. "That darned pup promised he'd listen to me. We got across the creek all right. The water was really roaring and it was scary, but he followed me and got across safely. But . . ."

"But?" Callie urged.

"Well, look for yourself."

The little white pup was covered from head to tail with mud. He was a gooey mess. He sniffed the pine needles without a care in the world. A little drop of mud plopped from the tip of his tail when it swayed from side to side.

"He hit every mud puddle between here and the rock hill. He even rolled in a couple of them. Chomps is fun to be with, but he won't mind worth a flip. Mama's going to be so *mad*. She'll never let him out again. When she sees what a mess he is, she'll—"

"Relax, Gray," Callie said, cutting me off. "They were so excited when they got back with the new car, they didn't even notice that he was gone. They even called the Garrisons to come over to look at it! All you have to do is get that pup back in his pen. They'll just think he got all dirty and muddy from the rain. You'd better hurry, though."

Chomps was still sniffing around the pine trees when I heard a car coming up the road. "Hurry, Chomps, get back in the pen before the company gets here."

Chomps had already found the new car and was sniffing the big tires. "What's that good smell, Gray?"

"Come on, Chomps. Here come the Garrisons!"

The silver Buick drove into the driveway, and the people stepped out. Mama and Daddy came from the house. Chomps was near the back of the new car.

Just as Mama opened the front door, Chomps jumped up and landed on the smooth leather seat . . . muddy feet and all.

CHAPTER 6

We got our first ride in the new Range Rover that day. Trouble was, we were in cages!

When Mama saw Chomps slopping mud all over the front seat of her brand-new SUV, she went crazy. She grabbed Chomps off the seat and put him back in his pen. She went to the barn and started tossing stuff around.

I ran to the garden and hid near the fence behind the bushes. When Mama finally came out, she had two big cages. She wiped the mud off the little dog and crammed him into one of them. Then she started looking for me. I flattened myself to the ground. I had a bad feeling about this. At first she called out, real sweet like, "Here kitty, kitty."

As time went by she began to call me by name. "Gray! Get over here, you mangy cat!"

If it hadn't been for Chomps's barking and looking

toward the bushes, I would have been safe. The little dog stood up in the cage and pointed his black nose straight at me. When Mama came toward the bushes, I tried to sneak off, but she was quick and grabbed me by the scruff of the neck. The first thing I knew, I was in the other cage, right next to Chomps. Mama shut the back door of her new vehicle and we were off.

"Gray, why didn't you warn me she was going to be so mad?"

"I've been warning you all day. Who thought you would jump on the seats of her brand-new car? What were you thinking?"

Chomps's ears were down against his head. "It smelled good. I wanted to see where the delicious odor was coming from. I didn't think they would take us away from our home."

I sat on my haunches as I nervously washed my paws and whiskers. "You've done it now. We're probably going to the pound or the vet. I told you to go back to your pen before they saw us. But, no, you had to leap in and get a good look for yourself."

"Gray, what are we going to do? I don't want to go away. I like it here with Mama and Daddy and you and Callie."

I batted at the door with my paws. I grabbed the metal with my teeth, but it wouldn't open. "There's nothing that I can do. We'll just have to wait and see what happens."

dust balls. Think straight, Cat! Rats are sneaky and mean, but they are just wimps. They try to look tough, but inside they are just a bunch of cowards. If they don't have control of the situation, they run. When they realize that they might be in trouble, they don't care who knows that they are afraid."

Callie puffed her chest out. She stood on the bed and looked at me. "You're a cat. Cats have to stand up to them. Cats aren't afraid of *anything*. Don't ever let those rodents know that you are scared. Look them in the eye, just like you did the mice when you were stuck with Flea on your head. You're getting bigger every day. You aren't a little kitty cat anymore. Just remember, 'Cats are afraid of *nothing!*'"

CHAPTER 4

Mama's voice made my ears perk up. It was still dark outside, too early for breakfast. On her way from the bedroom, Mama stopped to scratch my ears. I stretched, then curled back into a ball on the couch. Mama carried Chomps to the back door and set him outside.

"I'm ready to go car hunting," Mama called to Daddy.

"Got anything in mind?" Daddy's voice came back from the bedroom.

"Don't you think we need a sports utility vehicle to help us with these bad roads?" Mama walked to the kitchen and started fixing their coffee.

Daddy's bare feet made a plopping sound when he came in to give Mama a hug.

"I'm not sure. If we could count on the roads

being good when it rains, it wouldn't matter. That creek needs a lot of work even if it doesn't rain this spring. I don't know why they haven't built that bridge across it yet."

"It's usually just a dry creek bed, though."

Daddy nodded. "Yeah, but if the water ever rises too much, it could really be a problem." He sat down at the table. "Maybe you should check on the Internet and see if you can get some information about SUVs. I don't think we can count on the county commissioner to fix the road before summer, and maybe not even then."

They sat down to drink their coffee. They only had a sip or two before Chomps started yapping and bouncing against the screen. Daddy picked up his cup and walked to the back door. Mama stepped up next to him. "That sunrise is beautiful this morning. Maybe we should get up early every day."

"It is a peaceful time of day . . . except for that dog!" Daddy opened the door, and the little fuzzball scooted in and ran around in circles on the kitchen floor.

Mama scooped him up and headed toward her office.

When I woke up from my little catnap, I could hear Mama tapping on her computer. Callie was headed for the cat bowl. I hopped down from the couch and followed her to the kitchen. There was nothing in the dish. Callie flopped on the floor.

"What's going on, Gray? Mama should have my food ready by this time."

I jumped up on the cabinet to see if Mama had just forgotten to put our breakfast bowl on the floor. There was nothing but coffee. I hopped down.

"Mama has Chomps in the office," I meowed. "I think Daddy went out to the field. Maybe we should remind Mama that *we* are hungry even if she isn't."

Callie and I headed for the office. The door was shut tight. The only sounds we could hear were the tap-tapping on the computer.

"Meow!" Callie and I both called at once. "We're hungry. Feed us!"

Suddenly Chomps's little black nose stuck out from under the door.

"Hey, pup, get Mama to fix us some breakfast!"

"She's busy right now. I'm keeping her feet warm."

I pushed my paw under the door. I tried to rattle it so that Mama would notice us. "MEOW!"

"Gray, stop that. I'm busy!" The door opened just a bit, and Mama let us in. Callie and I both stared up at her.

"MEOW," we both howled.

"My goodness, what time is it? Just give me a few more minutes and I'll get you fed." Mama sat down and started to tap on the computer again.

Callie curled up on the floor near the door. I wanted to see what Mama was doing. I jumped on

The little dog whined as we drove down the road. I finished my bath and tried to relax as we continued our ride. It was no use.

When the car finally stopped, Mama picked up my cage, and Daddy carried Chomps's inside a brick building.

"Hi, Amy. We've got two wild animals for you. It seems that they can't stay close to home and have managed to make messes of themselves. Gray needs a flea bath and Chomps needs something. Can you help us?"

A pretty face peered into my cage. "Hello, sweet kitty. What have you been doing to get yourself into so much trouble?"

She looked into Chomps's cage, smiled, then opened the door. She pulled him out gently. "What a precious pup! I haven't seen a white Scottie in a long time. He's wonderful!" Chomps smiled back at her. The sweet tone of her voice made him wiggle so much I thought he was going to knock himself apart.

The woman looked up at Mama. "They don't seem too wild. I think we can get them under control again. Do you want a puppy cut for the little guy or do you think he's ready for a grown-up look?"

"He thinks he's grown-up. He might as well look like a big dog. Give him the works."

Mama and Daddy walked out. I pushed my face against the door of the cage to see where they were going. Mama and Daddy got into the big car and

drove away. I tried to figure out what I was going to do next.

"Okay, Chompers, I have to put you back until I finish Rosco here. We'll get to you pretty quick." The girl called Amy shoved Chomps back into the cage and rubbed his face before closing the door. She pushed our pens closer together.

A big black dog stood on a table at the back of the room. He held himself tall and proud. Amy took clippers and started snipping the hair off the dog. She left big pompoms of curly fur around the bottom of his legs, his tail, and around his chest. She took a white hairdryer and fluffed him all over. Then she put a big red bow in his hair and painted his toenails with *red* fingernail polish.

"Are you watching, Chomps." I snickered. "That's what you're going to look like when she finishes with you." I stretched out and folded one paw over the other.

"No way! Nobody is going to do *that* to me! That dog looks silly. I am going to growl and bark so that she will leave me alone."

"Jeff, will you get Gray and put him in the dip?" Amy called to the man in the back.

"Sure thing. Come here, Gray." A dark-haired young man with a black fuzzy caterpillar on his upper lip peeked in at me. I scooted back and watched him. He bent down to see where I had gone. I decided it was hair on his upper lip, because

it didn't try to run away even when he talked.

"Come here, kitty."

I hissed at him. He just smiled and said, "Ah, come on Gray. Be a sweet kitty."

Before I even had time to blink, his huge paw darted in and grabbed me by the scruff of the neck and pulled me out of the cage.

"Come on, kitty. This won't be so bad." I couldn't escape without using my claws, and I was already in too much trouble to try that. So I just dangled there in midair.

After Amy put the big dog in a cage, she went after Chomps. Jeff took me to a big bathtub full of water. I hate water! I began to squirm even harder. Jeff just held on tighter and plopped me in the tub.

"MEOW!" I howled!

Jeff took a cup and poured water over my head and back.

My hair was dripping and I was miserable. I couldn't get my ears to stand up straight. My whiskers drooped. He put some stuff onto my fur and started rubbing it all over me. Getting rubbed was okay. If I hadn't been so soggy and wet, I might have enjoyed it. Finally he rinsed me off and put me back in the cage. I shook myself and tried to get dry.

Before I could even get my whiskers straightened out, Amy took me from the cage. The hairdryer made a loud whizzing sound. I didn't like that. It blew hot air in my ears and made them twitch and

wiggle. I didn't like that, either. Amy rubbed and fluffed me. That wasn't too bad. Then she got a soft brush and stroked from my ears to the tip of my tail. That felt pretty good. In fact, it almost made me forget about the noisy hairdryer. When I was finally dry, she clipped the ends of my long claws. I didn't care for that, but it didn't hurt at all. Then she took tiny rubber bands and tied them onto my hair. One was right above my eyes and the other was near my tail. I couldn't see what was on my head, but a bright pink bow was attached on my other end. Once back in my cage, I grabbed with my teeth trying to get it loose. I spun around until I was worn out. It was stuck tight.

I flopped down and looked out the end of the cage. Chomps was on the table, and Amy was clipping his hair just like she had the big black dog.

"Told you so . . ." I meowed to Chomps.

"This isn't so bad," Chomps yipped at me. "She is very gentle, and I like the feel of the clippers on my skin. Besides, now Mama can't pull so much, when I get burrs in my fur."

"Don't look now, dog, but she is leaving a bunch of hair along the bottom, where you usually get burrs anyway."

"I don't care. This feels good." Amy used scissors to clip the fur on his face. She left lots of hair across the top of his eyes and around his mouth.

Amy whispered sweet doggie talk to him while

shoulder against the cage. Mama touched my head with the tips of her fingers. "Let's get home, kids."

When we got to the house, Mama put my cage on the ground and opened it so that I could step out. She carried Chomps's cage to the backyard. Daddy had found the place where we dug under the fence. Big chunks of rock filled the hole.

When Mama finally let Chomps out, I couldn't believe my eyes. Even though he had lots less hair, he somehow looked big and fluffy. He had a cloth tied around his neck. He had a matching bow tied in his tail.

I had to laugh at the sight before me.

"I don't know what you're laughing at, Gray. You've got a big pink bow right in the middle of your head. It matches the one in your tail." Chomps sat down with his back half. His front legs were still straight. His tail wagged behind him. I tried to look at the pink bow on my head. I reached up with my paw trying to shake it loose. It was stuck tight. I couldn't get to the one on my tail. I shook my body and walked around to the front porch. I needed a real catnap.

Callie peeked open one eye when I was almost to the swing. "What happened to you, Gray?"

I hopped up on the chair and stretched out. "Nothing. Why?"

"You look nice with the pretty bow in your hair. Have you been to see Amy and Jeff?"

"Yeah. How did you know?"

"I've been there before. They were nice to me. Were *you* nice to them, Gray?"

"Of course, I was nice. What are you thinking? I have manners. I know how to act."

"Well, you sure look pretty." Callie smirked at me.

I hopped off the chair. This was bad. I smelled funny, I had bows in my fur, and Callie was making fun of me. I decided to go out in the pasture to roll in the dirt. On my way past the barn, a snickering and giggling sound stopped me dead in my tracks.

Two mice stood there. One pointed at me and held the other paw over his mouth. The other held his stomach. It was more than I could take. Ears flat against my head, I charged them. I couldn't do anything about Chomps making fun of me, and I couldn't do anything about Callie's smart remarks— but *no way* was I taking this treatment from a couple of scrawny rodents!

When the two saw me racing for them, they darted through the crack in the barn door. I chased after them and squeezed through. Then . . . I stopped. The two mice were no place to be seen. But the Mama's new car was in there. She was so proud of it, I guess she decided to keep it inside and out of the weather. What stopped me was the sound. It was a scraping, scratching, gnawing sound.

It came from under Mama's new Range Rover.

CHAPTER 7

I scrunched down so that I could get a better look under the Range Rover. The scratching sounds continued, but I couldn't see a thing. I crept slowly toward the vehicle to get a closer look. I blinked. My eyes narrowed as I tried to adjust to the darkness. The gnawing sound got louder. I twisted my neck to look under the big car.

The fur on my back and tail fuzzed up as the big rat, Nora, dropped to the ground in front of me. She started laughing and pointing.

"Where have you been, Cat? You look ridiculous. Look at that big pink bow on your head." Nora's nasty laugh made me back away from the car. "Hey, guys, look at this silly cat!"

Suddenly several sets of yellow eyes appeared near Nora. "Yeah, I remember that little kitty. He's been in here before, but he never stays very long. Looks like he's been to the beauty shop." The gray one moved even closer.

Several rats appeared in the rafters. Each one had a remark to make about the bows in my fur. I backed away, then quickly turned and ran out the door. Their jeering laughter followed me like a cloud follows a thunderstorm.

Amy had told me that I was a pretty kitty. It felt good to be praised and taken care of, but here in the barn with the nasty rats I only felt embarrassed and uncomfortable.

As soon as I got outside in the sunshine, I tried to pull the bows off again. They were impossible to move. I strolled to a safe spot near the apple tree. I found some dust to roll in. I flipped to my back and tried to scrape the bow off. It felt good to roll around. I stood up, shook, and swished my tail.

Just as I was beginning my bath, I heard a whistle. It sounded kind of familiar. Sometimes when Mama got all dressed up to go someplace, Daddy would whistle at her and tell her how pretty she looked. She would always smile and give him a big hug. It was the same whistle, but different somehow. I looked toward the house to see if I could see Mama or Daddy. The whistle came again. Daddy was no place in sight. The sound was close. I perked my ears and tried to find out what was making the noise. Just then I heard a familiar laugh. With a jerk of my head, I looked up. There on the branch of the apple tree was my friend Flea.

I scampered up the tree trunk to the first limb where the mockingbird sat.

"Flea! I'm so glad that you are back. I have missed you!"

"Hey, Cat. You look really cute. Did you get all prettied up for me?" The bird fluffed her feathers.

"No, Chomps and I got in trouble and we had to go see Amy and Jeff. Chomps got a haircut and I got a bath and a wonderful rubdown." I purred just remembering.

"Who's Chomps?" The little bird stared at me.

"Chomps is the new dog. He's pretty cute. I'm trying to teach him how to hunt. Remember when I had to teach you?"

"That wasn't too long ago. I have gotten to be a good hunter this winter. Right now it's time to start looking for a place to build my nest."

"What about this apple tree? That is where you were born. Wouldn't that be a good place to start your family?" I tried to sharpen my claws on the bark of the tree.

"Mama may come back here. If she does, then she gets to make her nest in her tree. I have to find a place that is just right for *me.*" Flea stretched out one wing and used her beak to clean her feathers.

"There are lots of trees around here. You will find a good one close by."

touch us gently with her beak. We spent hours playing the game. Chomps would bark and bark as he
raced across the yard chasing the swooping shadow.
I would hide behind the trunk of the tree and leap
out just in time to touch the dark spot in the grass
as Flea flew past. It kept Chomps and me from getting very far from the house, so we weren't in trouble with Mama.

Other mockingbirds began to come back. Flea was
still looking for a perfect place to put her nest. Every
day she would check new trees searching for the
ideal spot to build her new home.

I was rubbing against the swing when I finally got
lucky and managed to get the bow off the top of my
head. The one on my tail was looking pretty ragged,
but it hung on. I don't know what Amy had done to
those bows to make them stay put for so long. My
smell was better, too. I felt more like a real cat. One
day, while Flea was away hunting for a place for her
nest and while Callie was taking a nap in the sun, I
mustered my courage to return to the rats' den.

Mama's big vehicle was parked in the middle of
the barn. The scrunching noises that I had heard
before were coming from under it. I squeezed myself
to the ground, my ears against my head. I wiggled
closer, a little bit at a time. The sounds grew louder
as I eased toward the car. My eyes were still adjust-
ing to the darkness when I saw Nora under Mama's

Range Rover. The big rat was chewing on wires beneath the car.

"Get out from under Mama's car!" I demanded.

The scrunching didn't stop. Nora just kept chewing and chewing.

"MEOW!" I howled.

Finally the noises stopped. "What do you want, little kitty cat?" Nora squeaked.

"Get away from Mama's new car. Go chew on some corn or something. You shouldn't be bothering stuff here."

"Stop me if you can!" The gnawing sounds began again.

I looked around to see if there were any other rats. My eyes narrowed to slits as I peered into the dim space. I couldn't see any ratty eyes staring back at me.

"Get away from Mama's car!" I demanded as I scooted closer.

Suddenly Nora dropped to the floor. She took a deep breath, making herself look very big and mean. "You sound like a pretty tough cat telling *me* what to do."

I took a deep breath trying to make myself look big, too. "You need to get away from Mama's car."

"Your mama needs to get *her* car out of *my* barn!" The rat moved closer to me.

I backed up just a bit. "This isn't *your* barn, you big rat! It belongs to Mama and Daddy."

Nora moved closer to my face. I could see her beady eyes glaring at me. Her whiskers twitched as she stared. "Get out of *my* barn, little kitty cat!"

I raised my right paw. Claws sprang out. Nora just smiled.

"Yeah, little kitty, come on. Reach over here with that paw. It looks downright yummy."

Trembling, I held my ground, but Nora didn't back away, either.

KAABOOOM!

The sudden noise sent Nora scurrying from under the car and up to the rafters. It sent me scurrying, too. I raced from the barn and out into the fresh air.

The wind shook the trees around me. Lightning seemed to be everywhere. I ran as fast as I could to the front door of the house.

"MEOW! Let me in!" I howled as loud as I could.

CHAPTER 8

Another loud clap of thunder echoed against the rock hill in the valley. Just as I scooted onto the front porch, Mama opened the door. I skidded between her feet, ran to the bedroom, and hid under the bed.

Lightning and crashing thunder kept me there. Hard rain beat against the windows. For a while I could hear the sharp sound of ice hitting the house, too. I remembered the day that Chomps and I had hidden under the rock cliff. This storm lasted longer and was much louder than the last one.

It was quiet when I finally pulled myself out from my hiding place. Callie was asleep on the pillow. The storm didn't seem to bother her a bit. She peered through half-opened eyes at me.

"Callie, didn't you hear that storm?" I asked.

"Sure, I did. Why?" Callie opened her eyes and stretched out her front paws.

"It was so loud. Didn't it scare you?"

"I was safe here in the house. It was noisy, but I wasn't worried about it."

"When Chomps and I got caught out in a storm, it rained so much that I almost didn't get that little dog back across the creek. Limbs, leaves, and twigs were everywhere. This storm was even more scary. I was inside and it was really loud!"

The old cat closed her eyes and seemed to be asleep again. I hopped off the bed. Chomps would talk to me.

In the office the little dog was asleep near Mama's feet. Mama reached down and picked me up when I rubbed against her leg. I sank my claws into the soft robe that she wore. She cradled me in her arms and gave me a good tummy rub.

"What are you doing, Gray?" I just purred at her. Nobody seemed to be very concerned about the rain, maybe I was just being a scaredy-cat.

When Mama finished with me, I headed for the kitchen to see if there was anything left in the food bowl. I could still hear the gentle patter of rain on the roof.

By the next morning the rain had almost quit.

"The weatherman says that there might be more storms later this week, so we should enjoy the sunshine . . . if it comes out today." Mama held out a cup to Daddy.

"I heard on the radio about possible floods. The western part of the state got even more rain than we did. The river is supposed to be out of its banks by noon tomorrow." Daddy sat down at the table and looked out the window at the sky.

Mama started stacking the dishes in the sink. "I'd better hurry and get to town. If they're worried about the river overflowing, then the low-water crossing on our creek may be a problem, too."

"I think that I will give our county commissioner a call." Daddy rocked back in his chair and folded his arms.

"He told me last year they would do something about it. The roads on his side of the county look like superhighways, but we're still slopping through the mud." Daddy picked up the little box on the wall and started pushing his finger at it. His eyes narrowed to tiny slits, just like mine did when I thought about Nora.

Mama headed for the door. "I'll be back as quick as I can."

I slipped out, hot on Mama's heels. I jumped up on the swing and stretched. I could hear Daddy talking to himself inside.

"Mr. King, aren't you ever going to get to this side of the county? I have seen some excellent roads on the east side. The road here is such a mess.

I don't think a grader can get through when it rains." Daddy opened the door and shoved Chomps out with me.

"I understand that you have the big bridge that you are working on. Yes, sir, I do know that school buses have to cross there every day. I understand that you have been working on *that* bridge for more than two years." Daddy's voice was getting louder.

Chomps put his front feet up on the swing with me. "Want to play?"

"Sure, let's get Flea and play tag." We started looking for the bird. I climbed four trees, before we finally gave up.

"Where do you think she is?" Chomps continued to sniff the bushes around the house.

"She's probably looking for a good place to build her nest. She has been checking for a while. I hope the place that she finally picks is close to the house. That way we can see her little babies when they start poking their heads out of the nest."

Just as we were headed back to the porch, Daddy came out and scooped us up. "You two better go to the backyard. I have to pull the hay truck out of the mud, and Mama will be pretty mad if you two take off. You've been such good animals, and I would sure hate for you to get in trouble again. Mama would be mad at *me!*"

Daddy carried us through the house and plopped

us on the back porch. "I'll be back pretty quick. Be good pets."

We heard Daddy start the tractor and head toward the road. Chomps and I walked along the edge of the fence watching for something to move so that we could practice pouncing.

I stayed in the yard with Chomps for a long time. We played chase. I climbed the big pine tree and waited for Chomps to come look for me. When he wasn't expecting it, I dropped from the tree and clunked him on the head and back with my paws. I took off before he even knew what hit him. He yapped and barked, then chased me round and round the backyard. We even took a nap under the picnic table. It seemed like Mama was taking a long time to get back from the store. I was even getting worried about Flea. She must have found a place for her nest and was working on it already.

The sun didn't come out, but it was warm and damp everywhere. I hopped over the fence and took a stroll around the place. The barn seemed quiet today. Mama Mockingbird was back in the apple tree and working on her new nest.

"Have you seen Flea today?" I meowed to the old bird.

"She was out in the trees just north of here," the bird cheeped. "Are you going to bother her, like you did me last year?"

I flipped my tail. "I didn't bother you *that* much.

Besides, I took care of Flea when she wouldn't fly away with the rest of the birds."

Mama Mockingbird wove pieces of straw in and out of her nest. "Maybe so, but you make Papa Mockingbird awfully nervous when you try to look in our nest. Please stay away."

I started to walk off. "I'll try to keep from climbing up, but I like to watch your little birds when they start to pop their heads out of the nest."

Strolling back toward the yard, I looked all around for Flea. Chomps and I would try to find her when Mama let us out later.

I jumped up and grabbed the top of the gate with my front paws. I pulled myself up and balanced there for a moment. Chomps wagged his tail when he saw me. "Shouldn't Mama be home by now? I didn't get any breakfast. I'm hungry."

It *had* been a long time since Mama left. It was hard to tell how long, because the sun wasn't anywhere in the sky. I looked around. Mama was taking too long. She said she would be right back.

"I'll go look for Flea and have her fly around. Maybe she can help us." I pulled myself back over the fence. Then I headed out north of the apple tree, where Mama Mockingbird had told me Flea was building a nest.

Meowing as loud as I could, I kept calling for my friend. I finally found her in a tall oak in the middle of the woods.

Flea whistled back at me. "Hey, Gray. What are you doing?"

"Would you go look for Mama? She was just going to be gone for a little bit, and she hasn't gotten back yet. Daddy took the tractor and left, so he's no help. Chomps is hungry and he's stuck in the yard. You're a lot faster than I am. You can look and see if she is on her way home yet." I watched as the bird continued working on her nest.

"This is my first nest, Gray. I have to get it just right. I'm sure Mama will be home soon."

"Please, Flea. I'm worried about Mama. It won't take you long. Just make a quick fly around to see if she is on the road somewhere. She's in the brand-new Range Rover, so she should be okay. If she was in that old car, it could be bad. Just check along the road for a couple of miles toward town."

"What if some bird comes along and gets my spot? I've been looking for this perfect place for a long time. I don't want to lose it. Other birds are coming here every day. If one of them sees what a great place this is, she might take my nesting spot."

"Tell you what, Flea, I'll climb up and keep your space for you. You haven't done too much to your nest yet. If I stay here, no bird will get your spot." I looked up at the fork between two limbs, where Flea had begun to gather her little pile of twigs.

"Okay. But don't you leave until I get back. Come on up."

I took a running jump, leaping to the base of the tree. Using my claws, I climbed to Flea's nest. I was careful not to touch the twigs. Flea had been working very hard, and I didn't want to mess anything up.

"I'll be back. You be here!" Flea was cranky now that she had found the spot for her nest.

"I'm not going anywhere. It's beautiful up here." From high in the tree, I could see Flea as she swooped toward the road that led to town.

Looking back at the house, I could see the apple tree where Mama Mockingbird was working on her nest. I could see the fence around the house. I could even see Chomps. Down the hill in front of the house, I could see the rock hill where Chomps and I had hidden from the storm. To the north was a small valley where cattle were grazing. The east side of the woods had more trees. I could see a little bit of pasture way beyond the forest, but mostly I saw limbs and branches.

I was still enjoying the view when I heard Flea's shrill cry.

"Gray, come quick! Mama is in trouble!" Flea swooped toward me as fast as a streak of lightning. Her eyes were big and round. "The Mama's car is in the water. The door is open, but I can't see her anywhere! Hurry!"

CHAPTER 9

I knew something was wrong. Mama should have been home a long time ago. What could have happened to her? She was so proud of her new car. Why would she leave it in the water?

I could hear Chomps growling and barking. "What's wrong? What's going on? Where's Mama?"

"Mama's car is in the creek," I meowed back as loud as I could. "I've got to help her!"

"Come get me out of the yard. I want to go, too." Chomps howled.

"Push your way through the gate like you did last time."

I heard the gate rattle.

"Gray, come back and help. I can't get through. The Daddy must have fixed it when we were at Jeff and Amy's. I can't get out!"

"I don't have time, Mama needs help right now!"

I ran down the driveway. Behind me, I could hear the little dog yelping.

Flea swooped off for the low-water crossing. She kept a straight path down the road. Running as fast as I could, I didn't even think about looking around to watch for cars. I was out of breath when I suddenly heard a thundering sound. Afraid that it might be a car zooming toward me from way back up the road, I moved to the ditch and stopped.

It was Chomps!

I had never seen him run so fast or hard. His little paws pounded the wet, hard-packed dirt, sounding like faraway thunder. "Let's go!" he barked as he raced past me.

Blinking my eyes, I yelled back, "How did you get out?"

"No time to talk. We've got to help Mama!"

We both raced off. Flea circled back to see what had happened to me. "Come on. We're almost there."

I thought we might see Mama walking back to the house. When we got to the crossing, we still couldn't see her anywhere. Chomps and I sniffed at the water where it flowed over the road. We could see her big car. The door was open and water was clear up over the wheels.

I stepped carefully into the dirty churning stream.

"She's not there, Gray. I've already looked." Flea landed on a small bush near the creek.

"I've got to see for myself."

"The water's running too fast," Flea chirped, flapping her wings. "Look at all the limbs and stuff floating down stream. It's too dangerous!"

The water was cool and swift as I moved into the creek. I had to see for myself. Mama had to be there! Just then the push of the swift current knocked my feet from under me. Frantically I grabbed for the bottom. It was no longer there. I paddled with my feet as fast as I could. The water didn't seem too deep, but I couldn't get a hold of anything.

I fought and struggled. The tumbling water pulled me under, but I clawed my way back to the surface.

Flea swooped overhead yelling at me. "Swim to the bank, where the water isn't as deep!"

Chomps ran beside the raging torrent. "Be careful, Gray!" he barked. "Please. You're scaring me. Get out! Get out of there—*now!*"

I didn't have time to meow and tell him that I couldn't get out. Every time I tried to open my mouth, water got in and I choked and sputtered.

As I paddled and clawed at the water, I suddenly began to feel colder. I couldn't get my feet to touch the ground for even a moment. My whiskers and ears were soaked. My body tumbled over some limbs. I could barely hear Chomps yapping at me. I felt like I was far, far away from everyone I knew. Deep water seemed to surround me.

I'd never been so scared. I'd never felt so alone.

Then, when all hope was lost—when I knew I was going to drown and never see my family again—suddenly out of nowhere, a giant paw grabbed me. I fought to get away.

"It's okay, Gray. Calm down." Mama's voice soothed me. "I've got you. You're gonna be fine."

Mama was in the water with me. She pulled me close to her body, then lifted me to a tree limb that hung out over the stream. Shaking my fur, I wanted to be as far away from that scary water as I could get. I made my way down the limb. But when Mama didn't follow me toward the bank, I stopped. Behind me, she leaned down until just her mouth and nose were above the swirling brown water. She pulled at her leg with both arms. Then she let go and raised her head so the water wouldn't get in her face.

"Meow! Let's go, Mama! We've been looking for you. We want to go home." Mama just seemed to ignore me as she tugged at something under the water.

I walked across the tree branch to the dirt. Frowning and worried, I looked back at her. *Why wouldn't Mama come with me? Why wouldn't she get out of that scary water?*

Flea landed on a small branch next to me.

"Why won't Mama come with us?" I asked.

Flea tilted her head one way then the other. "I think she is stuck," Flea chirped. "She keeps pulling at something under the water, but it's so muddy, I can't tell what it is."

Chomps ran up to me. "What's wrong?" He barked. "Why won't Mama come with us?"

"She's stuck! She can't get out!" I felt my eyes flash, as big around as my milk saucer. "We've got to get some help!"

"We can't leave Mama here by herself," Chomps woofed.

"Somebody has to get Daddy." Flea waved her wings and jumped up and down on the small branch. "We can't help her by ourselves. We're not big enough to do anything."

Flea scouted the fields for Daddy. When she got back, she led us down through the hayfield toward the rock hill. But we couldn't cross the creek. Even the big log where Chomps and I always crossed was under water.

"How can we get to the other side?" I meowed.

"There's an old wood bridge at the edge of the hayfield. I saw it when I was hunting for the Daddy. It's out of the way, but it was dry when I last checked," Flea said.

It took forever to get to the little wooden bridge. Water lapped at the bottom of it, and even splashed up between the cracks. Chomps and I never slowed down.

"We've got to hurry." Chomps panted. "The water is getting higher."

In the distance we could hear the rumble of Daddy's tractor.

Chomps and I were covered with mud. The little dog had a couple of sharp stickers in his paw. He never slowed down. He just kept running beside me.

Water puddles covered the field. Finally we could see Daddy's tractor pulling the old wagon toward us. He drove very slowly, looking back at the trailer. I stood in the path—smack-dab in front of the huge tractor. I meowed as loud as I could. But at the last second I had to jump to the ditch so he wouldn't hit me. The enormous wheel just missed the fur on the tip of my tail. Following behind, I meowed and meowed and meowed. I guess he didn't hear me. He never looked back.

Chomps barked at him. Daddy didn't seem to hear him, either. Chomps even ran up and bit the big round tires.

Daddy just kept driving.

Flea swooped back and forth in front of the trac-tor. Then she flew beside it for a little ways. Daddy didn't even look our way.

It was hopeless. No matter what we did, no mat-ter how much noise we made, he still couldn't hear us over the roar of the tractor. Chomps was so tired and out of breath that his tongue almost dragged on the ground. I huffed and wheezed, trying to catch my breath. Even Flea was tired. She fluttered down to land on a fence post.

Mama needed help. Daddy was the only one who could help her. We had to get his attention. We had to do something!

CHAPTER 10

What can we do?" Chomps sniffed. "I'm so scared for Mama."

I nodded my head, agreeing with him. "Me, too. If we could just get Daddy to stop the tractor . . . just for a second . . ."

Flea leaped from the fence post and swooped into the air.

"I'll stop him!"

Flea took a flying swing toward the sky. She dived almost to the ground, right in front of Daddy. Then she did it again. Up and down, back and forth, she swooped.

Flea finally whacked Daddy on the head with her beak. Her first snap wiggled his cap just a little. Even more determined, her second whack almost knocked Daddy's cap off. He had to grab it to keep it on his head. Frowning, he pulled it off and looked all around.

When Flea hit him again, she got him right on the bald spot at the back of his head. He yelled, leaped up from the tractor seat, and started waving his cap all around. Flea landed on the very front of the tractor and chirped as loud as she could.

Daddy leaned over the steering wheel and swung the cap at her. When he saw he couldn't hit her and when she didn't move or fly away, he turned the big, noisy machine off so he could hop down and go after her.

The instant the tractor stopped roaring and rumbling, Chomps raced toward him. He barked as loud as he could. I yowled at the top of my lungs.

Cap clutched in his hand and ready to swing at the mockingbird, Daddy finally stopped and looked at us. "What is going on? You two are in serious trouble. What are you doing here?"

Chomps howled. Daddy cocked his head to the side and frowned at him. Chomps growled in his deepest voice. Meowing, I raced up to Daddy and tugged on his pant leg with my claws. He shoved me aside with his foot. But I came right back.

"What's with you two? What's all the noise?" Daddy asked as he reached down and picked me up. He smiled and rubbed my fur. "You guys must really be lonesome today. What are you doing all the way down here?"

Chomps started bouncing around, then began run-

ning down the road toward where Mama was. Flea fluffed her little wings, then she made a huge screeching sound. I struggled to get away from Daddy. I jumped from his arms and landed near the front of the tractor.

"Meow! It's Mama!" I howled.

"What is going on? I don't have time to play, right now. I've got to get this hay out of the field." Daddy turned and started back for the tractor.

Suddenly I heard Chomps growl again. He wasn't very far away, trying to lead Daddy toward the bridge. When he heard him say, "I don't have time to play," Chomps spun around and charged.

Daddy's eyes flashed as big around as his tractor tires when Chomps grabbed his pant leg. The pup growled—as mean as he could—then shook Daddy's pants so hard I thought he was going to yank them off. Daddy's mouth flopped open.

Chomps let go. He spun around and raced toward the bridge, barking every step of the way. I chased after him, stopping now and then to look back.

Daddy followed us.

I didn't know Daddy could run. After all, he *was* a people and he only had two legs. Besides that, he was kind of old, too. But I was very proud of him and the way he kept up with us. Flea made big circles around us until she was sure we were all headed in the right direction. Then she flew ahead to go check on Mama again.

Daddy followed us, at a run, all the way across the bridge and up the road. But at the driveway to our house, he stopped. He coughed. He bent over and put his hands on his knees. Then he coughed and gasped for air again. Then . . .

Then he started up the driveway toward the house.

"Where are you going?" I yowled. "She's not at the house. It's this way. This way!"

Daddy had his cap off so he could wipe the sweat from his brow. Flea stopped him. She whacked him on his bald spot again. He waved his cap in the air and called her bad names. Then Chomps growled and charged.

Before he got there, Daddy turned and started following us once more.

"Okay. Okay, I'll follow you." He put his cap back on and shook his head. "I can't believe this. I've been chasing a dog, a cat, and a bird for almost a mile. I wish I knew what in the world was going on."

When we finally got to the low-water crossing, Daddy knew what was going on.

The second he saw Mama's Range Rover, he started out into the fast-moving stream. Flea clunked the bill of his cap with her hard beak. Chomps yanked on his pant leg. He looked around and the three of us raced down the creek bank. Daddy followed.

With my sharp ears I could hear Mama yelling.

We had to get a little closer before Daddy could hear. The moment he did, he began running. When he finally saw her, he ran even faster. He ran so fast that he shot right past me and then past Chomps. Flea was the only one who beat him to Mama.

Then, my heart sank when I saw what he did next. Daddy jumped into the water.

Mama yelled, "NO!"

Chomps barked.

Flea squawked.

I meowed.

Daddy just jumped in anyway. He hugged Mama in his arms and tried to lift her. She flinched and yelled. Daddy felt around, under the water, with his hand. Then he took a deep breath. It scared me even more when he went under the water.

But when he came up, Daddy had a big log in his hand. He lifted and shoved and pushed until the log turned, then tumbled out into the swift current.

When Mama was finally free, she pulled herself toward the bank. Daddy climbed up right behind her.

"How did you know where to find me?" Mama leaned against a tree and rubbed her leg.

Daddy nodded toward me and Chomps. "These two. Never saw anything like it in my life. You talk about weird . . . They made me follow them. There's a bird . . ." Daddy stopped talking and looked around in the trees. When Flea chirped, he smiled and pointed at her. "I think the bird was in on it,

too. But for the life of me, I don't know what a mockingbird is doing with Gray and Chomps." Daddy turned to Mama and smiled. He gave her another big hug. "Anyway, they brought me right to you. I guess they knew you were in trouble." He took her hand and gave it a gentle tug. "Come on. Let's get you back to the house."

When Mama looked at us, she smiled. It was one of the sweetest smiles I had ever seen. "Come on, Gray and Chomps. You're going to get treats today."

"What about me?" Flea chirped.

As soon as we got back to the house, Mama went to the refrigerator. She got a really big piece of steak and cut it up into little bite-size pieces. She gave half of it to me and half to Chomps. Before she took a nice, hot bath, she got some birdseed out of the bucket by the front door and put it in the feeder on the pecan tree.

While Mama was taking her bath, Daddy went to the box on the wall and started punching at it with his fingers.

"Hello." He held the box by his ear and started talking to himself. "Yes, this is Owen Priddle. We need a wrecker four miles west of town. We've got a Range Rover stuck in a low-water crossing. It's brand-new and it shouldn't have stalled out. Okay, I'll give you about twenty minutes, and then I'll meet you there. No problem. Thanks." Daddy put the little box back on the wall. Mama came in just as he hung it up. Daddy hugged her again and gave her a little kiss on the cheek.

"I've got to go see what happened to the car. They said that they would be here in about thirty minutes. That thing shouldn't have stalled out. It's brand-new. I'll be back."

Mama let Chomps out in the backyard to sleep in the sun. I went to the bedroom and told Callie what had happened. She moved so I could have her pillow for a catnap. Callie never gave me her pillow before. I guess she was very happy that we helped save Mama.

"Rats!"

The word snapped my eyes opened. I sat straight up on the pillow and looked around. "Rats!" the voice said again. It came from the other room. I was instantly awake. I sprang from the bed and trotted to the living room.

"The only thing we could see under the vehicle were some bare wires pulled down," Daddy told Mama. "When they hit the water, it must have shorted out the whole electrical system. It had to be a mouse or a rat. Chomps doesn't get out in the barn anymore. Gray wouldn't pull down wires. It just had to be one of those barn rats."

My ears perked up. I knew who had chewed on those wires. I remembered when I had seen Nora in the barn messing around under Mama's car. That was what she had been doing!

It made me so mad, I couldn't even see straight.

The next morning when Mama opened the front door, she let out a little scream and yelled for Daddy. "What in the world is it?" she asked when he got there. "Is it a gopher or an opossum?"

Daddy frowned down at the trophy I had left on the doormat.

"It's a rat!" he gasped. "A big one, too!"

I lay on the porch swing and smiled over at them.

"It's Nora," I meowed softly. "What she did to Mama was wrong. It was bad. She'll never hurt Mama again. The others won't bother us, either. They all ran away. I'll never let them come back."

It was a good trophy. Mama didn't even curl her nose or scold me when she picked the mat up and dumped the rat out in the field. She just hugged me in her arms and rubbed me. That night Daddy cooked steaks on the charcoaler.

I could get used to steak. It was even better hot than out of the refrigerator.

ABOUT THE AUTHORS

BILL WALLACE grew up in Chickasha, Oklahoma, a town of fourteen thousand people. He had lots of pets—dogs, cats, snakes, and lizards. He played baseball and football with his friends. His mother taught high school math.

CAROL WALLACE grew up on a dairy farm. They had lots of barn cats and two cats that got to come inside. She played with her dog Pooch, swung from the rope in the hay barn, and had her own special place on the rock hill. She attended a small rural school through eighth grade and then went to Chickasha High School. Her math teacher just happened to be Mabel Wallace. The first time Carol saw Mrs. Wallace's son, Bill, he was playing his trombone in front of the high school.

Bill and Carol hold master's degrees in elementary education from Southwestern Oklahoma State University. They are both authors and public speakers. This is their third book together.